ONE
CANDLE

ONE CANDLE

AND OTHER FOLKTALES
Compiled by the Editors
of
Highlights for Children

CONTENTS

ONE CANDLE

A Turkish Folktale
Retold by Olga Sharp Steele

"I can drink coffee straight from the boiling pot," said one of Nasreddin Hodja's friends.

"I can swallow a pound of ice," said another.

It was winter, and they were all sitting around the small tables in a warm coffeehouse.

Nasreddin thumped his fist on the table. "You know I can drink my coffee hotter than any of you. And if you can swallow one pound of ice, I can swallow two pounds!"

The other five men looked at each other.

"Perhaps you don't feel heat or cold at all," suggested one. "Not even the cold on a night like this."

"Of course I feel heat and cold," answered the Hodja. "It's just that I can control my mind. Why, I could stand in the cold and snow all night without any fire to warm me." He took a great gulp of sweet, black coffee.

"But you wouldn't try it on a night like this, would you?" asked one.

"Any night, any night," answered Nasreddin. "Just set the night. However cold, if I have so much as one candle to warm myself by, I'll—I'll give a feast for all of you."

This boast of Nasreddin's was what his friends had been waiting for. "Tonight's the night then," they all said together. "We'll come to your house tomorrow evening for dinner. Ha, ha." They put on their heavy coats and fur caps and set off for their warm beds.

Nasreddin shook his head at their departing backs. He put on his coat and cap and mittens and stepped outside.

The coffeehouse manager—his name was Ali—turned the key in the lock. "I left a candle burning inside," he said. "May it warm your spirit. *Allaha ismarladik.*" He set off for home, too.

"*Güle, güle,*" Nasreddin called after him.

Nasreddin stood alone in the market square. The night was dark and still except for the whisper of falling snow. He laughed to himself. There would certainly not be a feast tomorrow night. He, Nasreddin the Hodja, could stand the coldest of temperatures.

The night got colder and blacker. The snow fell thicker and thicker. Nasreddin shifted from one foot to the other. He stamped his boots in the snow. He beat his arms together.

The snow covered his fur cap. It covered the shoulders of his coat. It sifted past his collar and tickled his neck.

Nasreddin stamped his boots again and again. He walked around the square. He fixed his eyes on the candle flickering in the window of the coffeehouse. The candle did help his spirits.

Morning came finally. Nasreddin heard the *muezzin* calling men to prayer just as the sun was coming up. He knelt in the snow to thank Allah for the new day.

Nasreddin's five friends were among the townspeople who came to greet him, *"Günaydin."*

"Günaydin, günaydin. There'll be no feast tonight," boasted Nasreddin. "I told you I could stand the cold. All night long I stood in the cold and snow."

"But you had a candle to warm yourself by," retorted one of the friends, "the candle Ali left burning in the window."

"Yes, yes," said another friend. "You lost the bet. A candle gives heat."

The Hodja looked from one friend to another. So he had lost his bet, had he? He made his cold lips smile. "All right," he said, "come to my house at sunset." He started home, cold and tired. He was thinking about the candle in the window.

Nasreddin slept most of the day.

At sunset, the call to prayer sounded loud over the town. Nasreddin knelt to pray. He was still on his knees when he heard his friends coming.

"Come in," he called. "The door is open."

The five friends took off their shoes and left them in a neat row outside the door.

Nasreddin shook hands with each of his friends. "*Hos geldiniz,*" he said.

"*Hos bulduk,*" they answered.

"Please excuse me," said Nasreddin. "Dinner is not quite ready."

"Take your time," said the friends. They sat down cross-legged on the floor. They were smiling. At last they were getting even with Nasreddin.

They waited. And waited. One man rubbed his stomach. Another licked his lips. They sniffed the air. They could hear Nasreddin in the kitchen, but there was no smell of food.

"I hope you are not hungry," called Nasreddin. "Dinner is still not quite ready."

"Perhaps I can help," offered one man.

"Fine," answered the Hodja. "You can all come to the kitchen and help me wait."

Looking at each other, the men scrambled to their feet and hurried toward the kitchen. They stopped just inside the doorway.

The Hodja was stirring something in the great copper pot that was usually set on a brazier of burning coals. Tonight the pot hung on a chain from the ceiling. The pot hung about three feet off the floor. On the floor under the kettle was one flickering candle.

"I started the cooking as soon as I got home. I'm sorry it is taking so long," said Nasreddin with a grin. He looked into the pot, stuck in a finger, and licked it. "It hasn't started to boil," he apologized. "In fact, it doesn't feel the least bit warm. But maybe we can eat before morning."

Susanna
and the
Green Stockings

By Betty Bates

Once upon a time, on a farm as big as my thumbnail, there lived two sisters. The younger sister, Hester, was lazy and vain. She left clothes scattered about the bedroom and never, never did her chores. Still, she was lovely to see. Her eyes matched the bluebells, and her hair matched the buttercups. She was betrothed to Terrell, son of the village mayor, who had given him a house, a cow, two sheep, a chestnut horse, and a piece of land.

"A pity you can't find a rich husband," said Hester to her sister. She ran a comb through her hair. "Pick up my nightdress, Susanna. I'm busy."

The elder sister, Susanna, was as virtuous as she was lovely. Her eyes were the color of hazelnuts, and what an enchanting, full mouth she had!

Now she hung up the nightdress. For she often hung up Hester's clothes in their tiny room at the rear of the farmhouse. She also fed the chickens, fetched water for the stewpot, and pined for Reuben, the village carpenter, who was kind and industrious but had only a hammer, a saw, and a bag of nails. Sometimes he whistled about the farm helping her father make repairs. He was a joyful prankster as well, with harmless tricks. But Susanna was so shy that when he spoke to her she rarely found a word to say.

Now Hester's marriage approached. "Hurry, Susanna," said Hester as Susanna stitched her wedding dress. "And remember, you're to wear green stockings at my wedding."

Green stockings? Oh, yes. For since time began, an unmarried elder sister had worn them to her sister's wedding.

"And dance in the hogs' trough," said Hester.

Dance in the hogs' trough? Oh, yes. For it was said that if she did, she would find a husband.

Susanna did not want to wear green stockings or dance in the wooden trough where the hogs drank, scattering water about. Yet she did so wish to marry Reuben.

On the wedding day, the village celebrated in the barnyard of the bride's family. Susanna moved among the guests in her green stockings, filling mugs with cider. Passing the poultry run, she nodded to chickens, ducks, and geese, and to Galahad, the merry little hog who had strayed in from the meadow. Soon she came to Reuben, who offered her a smile. "Good day to you, Susanna."

Surely he was happy to see her. She must think of a pleasant reply. But all she could do was fill his mug.

How would she ever marry him as long as she was so timid?

After the wedding feast, the fiddlers struck up a tune. "It will soon be dark, Susanna," said Hester. "You must dance."

Susanna sighed, pulled up her long skirts, and carefully stepped over the mud into the hogs' trough. She spun and spun, as hands clapped, chickens clucked, ducks quacked, geese honked, and Galahad squealed.

Susanna was dizzy. All at once she stumbled, tripped, and fell into the mud.

The fiddling, clapping, clucking, quacking, honking, and squealing stopped.

Reuben leaned over her. "Susanna, are you all right?" he asked.

"Oh, yes." She sat up. As Reuben helped her to her feet, everyone breathed a sigh of relief. Still, she was covered with mud.

The fiddlers struck up another tune.

"Are you quite sure you are all right?" asked Reuben.

"Yes. I mean, no. I must look as if I fell into the stewpot. You'll not catch me in that trough again." Never before had she made such a long speech to Reuben. She felt shy no more. She sat firmly on the edge of the trough, pulled off her shoes, and flung them over her left shoulder. Galahad chewed on them in the mud. She tore off her stockings and flung them over her right shoulder. "What a trial it is to have a younger sister!"

"So you finally lost your temper," said Reuben. "Time you did. Shame on Hester, to make one so pretty dance in the trough!"

"Of course, it *is* the custom."

"I say it's a rotten one." He snatched up the stockings just as Galahad was about to eat them. "Let's play a trick on Hester, one that will hurt only her pride."

He took Susanna's hand, and they hurried to the back of the farmhouse. Reuben dove through the open window of Susanna and Hester's room, where Hester had left clothes strewn about. By the torchlight, Susanna could see that Reuben dropped the green stockings onto the chair and tossed Hester's under the bed. He hid the unlighted candle in a drawer and climbed from the window.

Hand in hand, they dashed to the front of the house. There stood Terrell with his chestnut horse. Hester was disappearing inside to change her clothes for the trip to her new home, as village youths and maidens shouted, "Hurry, Hester."

Soon Hester came running out in her homespun dress. Terrell snatched her up, set her astride the horse, and pulled himself up behind her. Gracious! In her haste to leave, and without a candle, Hester had put on those muddy green stockings.

"Look," said a youth, pointing and laughing.

"Yes, look," said the others, joining in the mirth.

"Susanna," wailed Hester, "how could you leave these where you knew I'd take them by mistake?"

"It strikes me that *you* were the careless one," cried Susanna.

Hester stared at her, struck dumb. At last she gave Susanna a wink and smile. "Well and warmly said, sister."

As the horse turned and clop-clopped away, Reuben grinned. "So, Susanna, you do know how to speak for yourself."

Soon she found herself dancing barefoot with Reuben, chattering gaily, as Galahad danced after them. Reuben and Susanna each reached down to clasp one of Galdhad's hooves, and those three danced together. All around the barn, the poultry house, and the hogs' trough they frolicked, splash-splash-splashing in the mud.

After Reuben and Susanna were married, Galahad came to live with them. And from that day forth, Susanna and Hester were as kind to one another as kind can be.

KEETE
AND THE
MAGIC SPEAR

Retold by Bonnie Highsmith Taylor

For a long time the people of the village at Sialook Bay had been hungry because there were no longer any fish in the waters. Every day the men would go out in their kayaks, but every night they would return with no fish.

Keete sat beside his grandfather, Tatmik, in front of the old man's lodge. Tatmik had not spoken for a long time, and Keete studied his face for a sign of what he might be thinking. Tatmik was a medicine man, and Keete hoped he would be able to save their people with his magic.

"Can you put fish back in the waters, Grandfather?" the boy asked at last.

The old man gave a big sigh. "No, Keete, I'm afraid not. I am very old and I am weak. My magic has also grown weak."

"But you were always a great shaman, Grandfather," said Keete. "None was greater than you."

The old man took the boy's hand and held it tightly. "That is true," he answered. "But, no more. No more—"

Keete turned his head away because he thought he saw tears in his grandfather's eyes. When he turned back Tatmik was staring at the ice mountain to the south of them.

Keete loved the great ice mountain but at times he watched it in fear, for on the other side of it lived two fierce and powerful giants, Ko and Agla. Though Grandfather had told him many times that it was not so, he thought the giants might climb over the mountain and destroy their village.

"They only harm those who come to their mountain," Grandfather had explained.

"Why do you watch the mountain, Grandfather?" asked Keete.

"Though my magic is growing weak," said Tatmik, "it tells me that there are many fish in the waters beyond the mountain." He looked deep into the boy's eyes. "We must go there, my grandson."

Keete drew back in terror. "But—but, Ko and Agla. They will kill us if we fish in their bay."

"If we stay here, we will die," said the old man sadly. "All of our people will die."

"But we will have to fight the giants, Grandfather," Keete cried. "You are old and weak, and I am so small I do not even own a spear."

The old man smiled at the boy. "I will give you a magic spear." He took Keete's hand. "Come, my grandson. We must cross the mountain and catch the fish in the bay to save our people."

They trudged slowly on for a long time. The old man leaned on the boy.

Several times Keete tried to ask Tatmik about the magic spear, but the old man answered, "You will know soon enough."

At long last they reached the top of the ice mountain. Keete's heart was beating wildly, partly from exhaustion and partly from fear.

Suddenly a piercing scream rang out. "AIEE! Who dares to come to our mountain?"

Keete moved swiftly to his grandfather's side. He trembled. "Quick, Grandfather," he cried. "Give me the magic spear."

Tatmik patted the boy's head. "Fear not, Grandson," he said.

"But they are coming!"

"Yes," spoke the old man. "It is Ko and Agla. They are equally strong and very jealous of one another."

"Please, Grandfather," pleaded Keete. "Where is the magic spear?"

"It is in your mouth," answered Tatmik.

Keete gasped in amazement. "W-what, Grandfather? What do you mean?" he sputtered.

"The magic spear, my grandson," the old man explained, "is made of words."

"Words!" cried the boy.

He could feel the icy ground quiver beneath his feet as the two fierce giants came nearer.

"Listen closely," said Tatmik. He whispered the magic into the frightened boy's ear.

"But, Grandfather—" Keete tried to protest, but by then the two giants were beside them, breathing down on the old man and the small boy.

Very calmly, the old man said, "You cannot harm us. We are protected by magic."

"Ha!" the giants snorted. "You have no magic. You are old and weak. Your magic is gone."

"Yes," said Tatmik. "That is so, but my grandson has a great magic. More powerful than mine ever was, because he is young and his magic is new."

"What magic is so strong that it will protect you from us?" asked Ko.

"It—it is a secret," Keete said in a near whisper.

"Speak up!" yelled Agla. "Tell us your secret!"

Remembering what his grandfather had told him, Keete said, as bravely as possible, "I can only tell my magic secret to one person. And that person must be the most powerful one in all the far north."

"Me! Me!" growled Ko. "No one is more powerful than I am!"

"Liar!" snarled Agla. "I am the most powerful!"

"I am!" replied Ko.

With that he gave Agla a shove. Agla gave Ko a shove. They lunged at each other. They fell to the frozen ground and wrestled about. Then they began to roll down the mountain. On and on they rolled, sliding and shouting. "I am the most powerful!" "No, I am!" Across the icy bar they slid. On and on and on—

When the giants were completely out of sight, Tatmik and Keete went down the mountain to the bay. After they had caught all the fish they could carry at one time, they started back to their village.

"Our people will fish in the bay beyond the ice mountain until the fish come once more to our waters," said the old man. "You have made this possible. You will be a great medicine man one day."

Keete smiled. He was very proud that he had learned the powerful magic of words.

Garlic Soup

Retold by Mary Ann Kuta

The wind shrieked around the corners of the tiny cottage, overwhelming the rhythmic click of Mother's needle. Pellets of ice hammered at the oilskin window.

Michal stared with a creased brow at his history book. "Vlasta said she must have that dress tomorrow, or you won't be paid."

Rubbing her eyes, Mother sighed. "I'll have it done." She stroked the fine fabric in her lap. "I've never made a dress as lovely as this."

"When I grow up, I'll buy you one that's even more lovely," Michal declared.

"Of course you will, but now you must learn your lessons."

A sharp knock came at the door. Michal and his mother exchanged glances. Who would be out in such weather? The knock came again, even louder this time.

Michal jumped up to answer. He slid back the bolt and opened the heavy door. A frail old man leaned against the door frame. He pulled his thin cloak tightly about his stooped shoulders and whispered, "Can you spare a morsel for someone who faints with hunger?"

Mother nodded.

"Come in," Michal said, quickly stepping back from the door.

Mother pulled a chair in front of the fireplace. "Sit down, Grandfather, and warm yourself while I prepare supper." She blushed. "I'm afraid we have but little to offer."

"Thank you, my dear. Anything is fine." The old man sighed with contentment as he stretched his fingers toward the fire. "You will not be sorry for your kindness."

While their visitor warmed himself by the fire, Michal watched his mother prepare a simple meal.

She broke off two cloves of garlic and minced them fine. Melting their last lump of butter, she fried the garlic until the bits were golden brown and their aroma filled the cottage. Then she added water and let the soup simmer over the coals.

"That smells good." Their guest smiled, nodding. Soon, deep breathing and occasional snores came from the chair.

While the stranger slept, Michal set a spoon and an earthenware bowl upon the table. His mother cut the last chunks of dark bread. Finally, she ladled the fragrant broth into the bowl. Tiny butter droplets formed circles of gold across the surface of the soup.

"Come, Grandfather. All is ready," Michal said, touching the old man's shoulder.

The visitor awoke with a start, blinking his eyes. He shuffled to the table. Placing both hands on the back of the chair, he drew himself up to his full height.

"My children." He spoke in a surprisingly clear voice. "Because you have been willing to share your last crust with me, I have a gift for you."

Gentle hands turned Michal and his mother toward the wall. "Close your eyes, and count slowly to one hundred. For every golden circle in this bowl of garlic soup, you will find a gold piece."

27

They followed his instructions carefully. When they opened their eyes, the stranger had vanished and the soup bowl was brimming over with gold pieces—enough gold to live comfortably for the rest of their lives.

Early the next morning, Michal delivered the finished dress, which was adorned with his mother's delicate needlework. Vlasta, the merchant's wife, snatched the dress eagerly. Trickling a few coins into Michal's hand, she dismissed him with a gesture. Michal couldn't resist telling her that this would be his last delivery. He explained their recent good fortune.

"Humph," Vlasta grunted enviously. "Some people have all the luck."

That same evening, while strolling by the merchant's house, Michal saw a familiar bent figure abruptly yanked inside. Was it so wrong that he stopped to peer through the front window?

"Sit, old man." Vlasta patted the back of a chair. "Try not to get it dirty. It's covered in fine damask."

Bustling into the kitchen, the merchant's wife dumped a large block of fresh butter into the pot with the garlic. She fluttered about, talking to herself. "I'll serve him richer soup than that seamstress could ever make—and more of it. More soup for him means more gold for me."

Vlasta laid her finest linen tablecloth on the polished table. She set a silver spoon and a huge china bowl in front of her guest, who was observing her with a cocked eyebrow. Last of all, Vlasta poured her garlic soup, great quantities of it, into the bowl and stood back, smiling expectantly.

Clearing his throat, the elderly visitor said, "My dear woman, you too should be rewarded in proportion to your virtues."

He stood up and walked to the back of his chair. "Turn around. Close your eyes and count slowly to one hundred."

Michal saw the old man struggling to suppress a smile that twitched at the corners of his mouth. He repeated the identical words he had spoken to Michal and his mother. "For every golden circle in this bowl of garlic soup, you will find a gold piece."

Chuckling with satisfaction, Vlasta shut her eyes and counted, slowly at first, then faster and ever faster. She whirled about and found one gold piece on the bottom of her china bowl. Just one gold piece.

"What happened, old man?" she screeched, stamping her foot.

But the visitor, whoever he was, had disappeared.

Michal judged it was time for him to leave also. He crept away, looking thoughtful.

In her greed, the merchant's wife had put too much butter in the soup. The grease had clung together in one huge circle.

Vlasta received one gold piece for one ring of butter—exactly what she deserved.

TOSHIYUKI
THE
STONECUTTER

A Japanese Tale

Retold by Bonnie Highsmith Taylor

Toshiyuki sat beside his hut and chiseled away at a huge stone. He was making a birdbath for a rich merchant's garden. As Toshiyuki chiseled at the stone, the hot sun beat down on him. His arms ached from holding the chisel tightly and swinging the heavy mallet.

Nearby, on a large mulberry bush, a small bird sang gaily.

"Why do you sing so?" grumbled the stonecutter.

"Because I'm happy," said the bird.

"Hah!" sneered Toshiyuki. "Foolish is more like it. Why should you be happy? You are not grand like the peacock. You are not mighty like the eagle. You are only a small, brown bird. You have no greatness."

But the small bird continued to sing on the mulberry bush.

Suddenly the emperor himself, surrounded by soldiers and courtiers, came riding down the road on a magnificent white horse. The people bowed as he passed.

Toshiyuki wiped his brow. "Oh," he sighed. "If only I were an emperor instead of a stonecutter."

The bird cocked its eye at Toshiyuki and said, "It shall be so."

And, wonder of wonders, Toshiyuki was an emperor. People bowed before him. He was surrounded by soldiers and courtiers. He rode along proudly, thinking, *How very great I am.*

But after a while the sun shining down on Toshiyuki made him feel faint. "What is this?" he muttered. "Is the sun more powerful than a great emperor? If so, then I wish to be the sun."

Instantly Toshiyuki became the sun. He sent his strong rays out over the land. "How magnificent I am," he cried.

But all at once a dark cloud blocked his rays.

"What!" he exclaimed. "A cloud is more powerful than the sun? Then the only thing for me is to be a cloud."

As a cloud, Toshiyuki could hide the sun and cause torrents of rain to fall on the earth. How powerful he was!

But then the wind decided to blow. It blew down trees and dashed water over the banks of rivers. And it blew the cloud all over the sky.

"That's for me!" shouted Toshiyuki. "I must be the wind! I must!"

Toshiyuki loved being the wind. He whipped the kites about the sky. He blew hats off people walking down the road. He roared through canyons.

Far, far below he spied a huge boulder. "I shall carry that stone across the sea," he boasted.

He took a deep breath and blew hard. The stone did not move.

"I do not understand," he said. "As Toshiyuki I could turn the stone into anything I wished. Is it possible that a stonecutter is as great as the wind, the clouds, the sun, and the emperor himself? I am the one who has been foolish. I wish to be Toshiyuki again."

And he was. Once more he sat beside his hut and chiseled at the stone birdbath, while the small bird sang gaily in the mulberry bush.

SIRENA
THE FISH GIRL
A Legend from Guam

Retold by Kathy Millhoff

Long ago when life on the Pacific island of Guam was peaceful and simple, there lived a happy young girl named Sirena.

Like all Guam girls, Sirena worked day and night to help her mother with the chores around the house. Most families were enormous in those times, and the cooking and the cleaning never stopped.

The job that Sirena most loved to be given was that of washing the family laundry.

Was it the fresh clean smell or the bright colors of the newly washed clothes that Sirena loved?

Not at all.

For, more than any clean clothes, more than any party with bananas fried in coconut milk, more than anything, Sirena loved the water. And she loved, in particular, swimming in the water.

And Sirena was never content with just a cool dip in a stream or a speedy dash into the surf. She loved to dive and splash and race with the fish— all day.

Day or night, rain or shine, Sirena could be found swimming.

She knew every river's bend and curve, every deep pool or shallow cove. She knew the rapids, and she knew the hidden streams.

If you had been there and heard people talking, you might have heard them saying, "That Sirena! She's a sweet girl, but she's always in the water, always swimming!"

Sirena had 11 brothers and sisters and dozens of cousins, aunts, and uncles. She had grandparents who told her fascinating stories of the old days and parents who taught her to care for the small children, to cook, clean, plant taro, and harvest breadfruit.

And, like every other Guam child, Sirena had a godmother, a *nina,* whose job it was to see that

Sirena grew up safe from harm—happy, healthy, loving, and protected.

"Sirena," her *nina* would say, "always obey your mother. Listen to her. Immediately do what she asks."

And Sirena tried to do what she was told, but always it seemed that the water sang to her, called her for just one more swim.

One brilliant blue day in June, Sirena's mother called to her, "Sirena, take the family laundry to the river and see that it's back here clean and dry by this afternoon. We have a party to go to tonight."

Sirena already knew about the party. It was a christening party for her cousin Mikaria's new baby daughter.

"I'll be back before you know I'm gone," Sirena happily called over her shoulder, as she raced to the river.

She was almost there when she remembered the dirty clothes she had left back at the house.

Finally, with the laundry swishing and swirling in the current, Sirena stared into the glistening water and wondered which of her new blouses she would wear—the blue or the yellow?

But, how the water sang out that day, calling her to jump in. Even darting fish seemed to beckon to her. "Come on, Sirena, just one little dip to cool off. The sun is becoming so hot."

Sirena actually managed to ignore her surroundings until midmorning. But at last, with the sun high in the sky, Sirena could stand it no longer, and she took a running leap from the rocks and dove like a dolphin beneath the surface.

Time passed. The sun began to set, but Sirena never noticed. She was involved in a confusing game of tag with the fish, swimming through the rocks.

"Sirena! Sirena, you come out now!"

It was her mother shouting from the rocks, waving a still unwashed skirt.

"Mother, I am so sorry," Sirena began, standing before her mother.

"Sirena, I have lost patience. If you wish to live like a fish, then from now on you are a fish!"

As soon as the angry words were out, Sirena and her mother were shocked to see Sirena's feet, then legs, begin to change to the tail and fins of a bright blue fish.

"No," her mother said, too weakly. The curse continued to change Sirena.

"Stop this curse now! No more!"

It was the voice of Sirena's *nina,* coming from just down the riverbank.

The *nina's* words stopped the spell, but could not change Sirena back into the girl she had once been.

From her waist downward, Sirena was a beautiful fish. From her waist up, she was still the sweet girl everyone loved.

"Daughter," her mother said.

"Mother," Sirena said, grinning. "Never be sad for me. I'll always be close by. I'll be swimming in a nearby stream or pool."

And with a bright flick of her shimmering tail, Sirena was gone.

From that day onward, Guam children always think twice about disobeying their parents.

But wherever on Guam there is a bright gleam of water or a brilliant slant of rainbow or a waterfall's silver spray, people are sure they have just missed seeing Sirena, splashing, chasing, and laughing with joy because she still races the fish through the ripples.

THE HOUSE THIEVES

A Korean Folktale

Adapted by C. Nordhielm Wooldridge

Years ago, in a small village in the Land of the Morning Calm (which you and I know as Korea), there lived a charcoal maker who was so poor that his only possession, besides the wooden hut in which he lived, was a large black kettle.

The charcoal maker was so worried the kettle might be stolen that he refused to let it out of his sight by day and slept in the bottom of it by night. All around him, the other villagers talked and laughed and played and worked. But the charcoal maker could not take part, because he was too busy worrying about his kettle.

"My son," said the wise old village grandfather, "you are letting worry about what *might be* take the joy out of what *is!*" But the foolish charcoal maker would not listen and continued to worry over his kettle.

One night, at a very dark hour, two thieves sneaked into the village and peeked inside each hut, looking for something to steal. But inside every hut lay a family asleep on the floor, and the cowardly thieves didn't dare enter for fear of waking someone.

The night was almost past, and the thieves were about to give up when they peeked into the charcoal maker's hut. Seeing no one, they crept inside. The only thing they found was a large black kettle—but even this was better than nothing.

So, having no idea that the charcoal maker was asleep in the bottom of the kettle, they tied ropes around it. Then they hauled it as quietly as they could out the door and down the dirt road that led away from the village.

"I have never known a heavier kettle than this one," grunted the first thief before they had gone far.

"And the sun is beginning to rise," answered the second. "The villagers will be up and after us before long." So they abandoned the kettle and ran for their lives.

Soon the charcoal maker began to feel the sun's warmth and light flowing in through the mouth of the kettle. He stood, stretched his crumpled arms and legs, and stepped out. His bare feet felt dirt and stones. He opened his eyes wide. Where there had once been walls, there was now air. Where there had been a roof, there was now sky. There could be only one explanation for all of this.

"My house!" he wailed. "My house has been stolen! *Aigo! Ai-i-i-go-o-o!*" And he melted into a sobbing puddle of despair.

Before the charcoal maker had wailed and sobbed for too long, down the road came the village grandfather on his morning walk.

"What is ailing you, my son?" he asked.

"Can you not see?" wailed the charcoal maker. "My house has been stolen in the night! All these years I have been worrying about my kettle, and now my house has been stolen from on top of me! *Ai-i-i-go-o-o!*"

"Ah! So it is with life." The grandfather sighed, but there was a twinkle in his eye. "While you are worrying about one thing, another thing sneaks up on you and happens."

"Yes, so it is with life," sobbed the charcoal maker.

"It makes one wonder if there is any use in worrying at all!"

"Yes, it makes one wonder," said the charcoal maker, sobbing not quite so hard.

"Better to look for the joy in today, and let tomorrow take care of itself."

"Yes, that is better," repeated the charcoal maker.

"Besides," added the grandfather, "if you continue to worry about your kettle, who knows what might be stolen next!"

"Yes, who knows?" agreed the charcoal maker.

The grandfather turned to walk back to the village. "On my way here," he said over his shoulder, "I passed a house that looked very much like the one stolen from you last night."

The charcoal maker could not believe his ears. He clumsily hoisted his kettle up on his shoulders and stumbled after the wise grandfather, who led him straight to his own house. It was standing in the usual place, but the charcoal maker did not notice. He only felt joy at having his house back again.

From that time on, the charcoal maker spent his nights sleeping beside his kettle instead of in it. He stopped worrying, and he began talking and laughing and playing and working with the other villagers. He lived a long life. His house was never stolen again, and neither was his kettle.

Maui
the Sun-Catcher

Retold by Bonnie Highsmith Taylor

Long, long ago, when the world was new, summer days were no longer than winter days— until Maui, a young Hawaiian boy, came up with a plan.

Young Maui sat on the ground twisting coconut fibers into rope. His father, Akalana, and his older brothers were going hunting and needed the rope to carry home their game.

His mother, Hina, worked nearby at her tapa board. Maui never tired of watching her, and when he turned his attention from his rope weaving to watch her, Akalana said, "Come, come, my son, you are wasting time, and time is short."

Maui's fingers moved fast, but he saw that his mother's fingers moved faster still as she worked the wet bark on her tapa board.

"How is it, my mother," asked Maui, "that you can move your fingers so swiftly?"

Hina smiled at her son. "Practice, Maui," she answered. "Practice."

"But I don't like you to work so hard," Maui said.

"I must make clothing and bedcovers for the family," said Hina. She sighed. "If only Sun did not move so fast across the sky. Before my tapa has time to dry it is dark."

Maui hit the ground with his fist. "A curse on Sun!" he cried. "I shall teach him a lesson!"

His brothers burst out in laughter. "And what will you do, oh mighty one?" they jeered.

"I will—I will—" Maui sputtered. "I—I will make him slow his journey so that our mother need not work so hard."

One brother scoffed, "You will send him into a rage with your foolishness, that is what you will do. He will turn you to ashes."

Akalana put his hand on his son's shoulder and said, "What you are suggesting is impossible, Maui.

Do not forget that Sun is a god and is very powerful. You are only a boy and no match for him."

With that the father and the brothers left Maui behind with his mother and went hunting.

For a long time Maui worked at braiding the coconut fibers into rope. Already Sun was over halfway across the sky, and Maui had only been up from his sleeping mat for a few hours.

At last his mother said, "Your father is right, Maui. You are no match for Sun. He will do as he pleases."

Maui looked down at the knife he wore in his belt. "If I could only reach Sun I would carve him into small bits and throw him into the sea."

"But then," said Hina, "it would be cold and dark forever."

Maui knew she was right. Was there no way he could make his mother's work easier? He shook his head sadly. "If only there was some way—"

Hina answered, "If there is a way, your grandmother, Kahu-akala, would know. Because she is ancient, she is very wise. Perhaps she might know a way."

Maui became excited. "Tell me how I may find her. For remember, I have not seen her since I was a small child."

Hina gave Maui directions to where the ancient Kahu-akala dwelled.

"On the next island is a very high mountain. Climb all the way to the top of the mountain, and you will come to a giant wiliwili tree. Under the tree you will see a small hut of grass. This is where your grandmother lives."

Maui told his mother good-bye and set out on his long journey, carrying his knife and ropes for pulling himself up the steep mountain.

It was early the next morning when Maui reached the hut under the wiliwili tree and found his grandmother. She was happy to see the boy, and after listening to his problem she pondered it for a long time.

Finally she spoke. "It might work. Because you are a brave boy, it might work."

"What, Grandmother?" Maui urged impatiently.

The ancient woman pointed to the fiber ropes that Maui had coiled over his shoulder. "Snaring Sun," she said. "I would wish for him to stay longer in the sky also. To warm my old bones."

"But how can I snare Sun?" asked the boy.

"Sun," explained Kahu-akala, "has eighteen rays, which are his legs. Just beyond is a crater known as House of the Sun. In a short time he will waken from his sleep and stretch his long legs, one by one, over the rim of the crater. You must set snares with your ropes before he rises. He will

48

rant and rave, but you must not set him free until he agrees to slow his daily journey."

How right his grandmother was.

When Sun stepped over the crater's rim and became trapped in the coiled ropes, he ranted and he raved and he roared.

Sun's hot breath bellowed in Maui's face. "How dare you! How dare you!"

Maui held the ropes tightly. "You must promise to travel more slowly across the sky," he shouted. "Only if you promise will I set you free."

"I will not promise anything!" roared Sun. "Why should I?"

"Because if you do not slow down your journey, my mother's tapa takes days and days to dry."

"Ha!" snorted Sun angrily. "What do I care?"

Maui gave such a mighty jerk on the ropes that Sun cried out in pain. "Okay, okay! I promise, I promise!" Then he added, "But for only part of the time. The rest of the time I will travel as I choose."

Maui agreed.

From then on, for one half of the year, Sun traveled slowly across the sky. There was plenty of sunshine to ripen the fruits of the islands, to warm the old grandmother's bones, and to dry Hina's tapas.

A PIECE
OF
GOOD LUCK

An Old Eastern European Fable

Retold by Susan Terris

Once upon a time, a farmer named Boris was plowing his field under the hot summer sun. Suddenly there was a loud clinking sound. His plow had hit something under the dirt.

Boris dropped the plow. "Oh, no," he cried out, "not another stone! I thought I had cleared every stone from this miserable field. Why do I always have such luck?"

Then Boris bent down to see what it was that the plow had struck. There in the dirt he found a shining gold coin. He just couldn't believe his eyes. "I must be dreaming," he told himself. "Gold in a field of potatoes? Impossible!"

Pulling out a large kerchief, Boris mopped his forehead. "It must be sunstroke," he mumbled, gazing down at the incredible piece of gold.

Boris dropped to his knees. He plunged his hands into the dirt. He found another coin and another. By the time Boris had finished digging, he had a hundred pieces of gold before him. And maybe a few more.

"Wait till my wife sees this," he said. But the more he thought about his wife and the gold coins, the more worried he became. "If I tell my wife," he reasoned, "she will tell the whole village. Anna is a good wife, but she talks too much. Then the judge will call me to court and take the money from me. He will think I have stolen the pieces of gold."

On the way home, Boris had an idea. He stopped in the village to buy a fresh fish and a freshly killed rabbit. He carried the fish and rabbit back to his potato field. Carefully he placed the rabbit in a tree and the fish in a leafy green bush. Next, he put the gold pieces back in the field and covered them with a great clod of dirt. Then he ran home to find his good wife.

"Anna, Anna," he called out. "Let's go out in the field and catch a fish for dinner."

Anna threw up her hands. She was quite sure that Boris was out of his mind. "Sit down, dear," she urged. "Have a mug of cold water. This hot sun has gone to your head."

But Boris wouldn't sit down. He nagged and pleaded until Anna agreed to come to the field with him to catch a fish for dinner.

Side by side they walked along through the freshly plowed field. Soon Boris stopped at a leafy green bush. Picking up a stout stick, he lunged at the bush. "I've got him!" Boris cried out.

And a large, scaly fish flipped out of the bush right into Anna's arms. Anna was amazed. "Fishing in a potato field?" she gasped. "We must both be out of our minds!"

"Look at that fish," Boris said as they walked on through the field. "Wouldn't it be grand to have a juicy rabbit to eat with our fish? Look up in that tree and see if you can spot a rabbit."

"A rabbit in a tree?" Anna asked.

"Yes, of course," Boris replied. He lunged at the tree with his stick. To Anna's amazement, a rabbit fell down and landed at her feet.

"Fish in bushes! Rabbits in trees!" Anna said. "What is the world coming to?"

Just then Boris kicked up a clod of dirt. There, shining in the afternoon sun, was a great pile of gold coins. There were at least one hundred coins. Or maybe a few more.

Carefully, Boris picked up the gold pieces and wrapped them in his kerchief. Then he took Anna's arm and led her home. She kept talking to herself about fish in bushes and rabbits in trees and gold in potato fields.

In a small village, it is hard to keep a secret. It wasn't long before everyone knew that Boris and Anna were no longer poor. Anna didn't tell more than one or two of her friends at the most, but soon everyone in the village was talking about the hundred gold pieces that Boris had found in the field.

Boris was right. It wasn't very many days until the judge called him to come before the village court. "See here, Boris," the judge said. "I want to know how you and your wife have become the owners of one hundred pieces of gold."

Boris looked up at the judge. "Pieces of gold?" he asked. "Who says we have one hundred pieces of gold?"

The judge frowned. "Come, come," he complained, "your wife has told the whole village that you have found a hundred gold coins."

Boris shook his head. "You're not going to believe my wife, are you? She's a good woman, but foolish. You can't believe a word she says."

The judge was angry with Boris. "Let this man's wife be brought before the court," he called out. "Then we shall find out about those gold coins."

So Boris's wife, the good Anna, was brought before the judge. "Tell me, Anna," he said, "has your husband found some money?"

"Why, yes," Anna replied. "One hundred gold coins. Or maybe a few more."

"Just when did this happen?" the judge asked.

Anna smiled. "Why, he found the coins the same day he caught a fish in a bush and a rabbit in a tree."

"A fish in a bush and a rabbit in a tree?" the judge roared. "Impossible!"

"But there was a fish in a bush! There was a rabbit in a tree," Anna insisted. "I was there, and I saw them with my own eyes."

"Take her away," the judge bellowed. "Take this foolish woman out of my court!"

Then the judge turned to Boris. "Go on," he said. "Go on home. I feel sorry for you, living with a foolish woman like that."

With a small smile on his face, Boris took hold of Anna's arm and led her home.

That night after Anna was asleep, Boris sat up and counted his coins. Yes, he had been right. There were at least one hundred. And maybe a few more.

The Secret of the Turtle Egg Soup

A Chinese Fable

By Marlene Richardson

Many years ago when China was called Cathay, there lived a man named Chin Li. He was well liked by everyone because he was wise, kind, and just. He earned his living by making a very delicious soup. The secret of its flavor was in the two eggs of the giant sea turtle that went into each pot of soup.

Chin Li could have become a very rich man if he had sold more soup. But years before when he had first found the secret place where the turtles laid their eggs, he had promised Turamin, leader of the turtles, that he would never take more than two eggs a day.

These were the days of the warlords, and life was very hard for the common people. In Chin Li's fiftieth year, the year of the tiger according to the Chinese calendar, his city was conquered by the warlord Changshi. Changshi was so cruel that everyone feared him. If anyone caused Changshi the slightest displeasure, he would put him in prison.

Changshi soon heard Chin Li made the finest soup in the city. He sent his guards to Chin Li's shop and ordered him to appear at the palace the next morning. Chin Li was petrified, but no one could refuse the wishes of this powerful ruler. So the next day Chin Li, quivering on the inside but holding his head high to hide his fear, appeared at the palace. Changshi was more terrible than Chin Li had imagined, with wild black hair and a fierce evil face.

"Ah, it is Chin Li, maker of the delicious turtle egg soup and the only man in Cathay that knows where the turtles lay their eggs. I have many banquets, and from now on you'll serve your delicious soup to my guests."

"Oh, most powerful Lord Changshi, I cannot do this because of the promise I made many years ago. If I were to collect enough eggs for many banquets, there would be none left for hatching. It would mean the end of the giant turtles. Turamin, the leader of the turtles, has trusted me these many years. I would be without honor if I betrayed him now."

The words of Chin Li threw Changshi into a terrible rage.

"You will obey my wishes, or curse the day you were born! Return to the palace tomorrow with the eggs for the banquet, or my soldiers will burn your shop and you and your wife will feel the full measure of my anger. Go! You have displeased me! Consider well your decision!"

Unhappy and frightened, Chin Li hurried home and told his wife what Changshi had said. She was a good woman, but the fear of the warlord was too terrible. Bursting into tears, she cried out:

"Honorable husband, we are doomed! Even the souls of our ancestors cannot help us. I fear I will not live to see the sons of my sons!"

That night sleep would not come to Chin Li. He walked down the beach. Feeling lonely and afraid, he called out into the darkness, "Help me, Turamin! Please help me!"

There was no sound except for the surf pounding on the shore. With a heavy heart he started for home. Wait! Was that something he heard over the sound of the waves? He stopped and listened. Yes, it was the turtles. He could see them swimming to shore, calling, "Wait, Chin Li! Stay!"

Running down to greet them, Chin Li quickly told Turamin the troubles that had befallen him.

"Fear not, my friend," said Turamin. "The sly fox can often outwit the fierce tiger. Do and say exactly as I tell you, and Changshi will fall by his own hand."

The next morning Chin Li went to the palace with a large basket of turtle eggs. Soon preparations for a feast were underway. At sunset the hall began to fill with guests. A loud gong announced the presence of Lord Changshi and the start of the banquet.

"Lord Changshi," said Chin Li, "I have prepared for you the finest turtle egg soup. But before it is served, I must warn you that these sea turtles are favorites of the gods. Therefore only the pure at heart may eat this soup with pleasure. If there be evil in a man's heart so will it cause pain, measure for measure."

"Silence!" roared Changshi. "Serve the soup."

Even as Changshi shouted those brave words, he was afraid. If they were true, his suffering would surely be terrible—and measure for measure! Could it kill him? He tried to eat the soup, but he was so frightened he could hardly swallow. Oh, the shame it would bring if his guests knew he couldn't eat the soup! There was only one way for him to save his dignity.

Quickly clapping his hands for attention, Changshi said, "Honorable guests, this soup is delicious. I love it! But I have given further thought to the words of Chin Li, and I have decided that he speaks with much truth. If we robbed the sea turtles of all their eggs for the pleasure of our banquet table, it would soon mean the end of the giant sea turtles. This would be a cloud on the honor of Cathay, for the gods made many creatures for humans to share this land with. As the most powerful of the warlords, it is my duty to protect these creatures. From this day forward it shall be the law that no man, be he rich or poor, shall ever ask Chin Li to collect more than two eggs, nor will they ask him to reveal the secret hiding place."

A very happy Chin Li returned to the quiet life of his soup shop. Lord Changshi, who for the first time in his life recognized the evil in himself, changed his ways and later became renowned for the justice and wisdom he showed in ruling all his subjects.

My Brother's Keeper

A Legend from Israel

Retold by Sue Brooke

Long ago there lived two brothers who were very poor. They lived in tiny huts at opposite sides of their large wheatfield. At the end of each summer, when harvest time came, the brothers divided the grain they had grown into two equal parts. Some of it they took to be milled into flour, from which they baked bread. The rest was sold for money, with which they bought shoes, clothing, and tools.

Although they toiled from sunup to sundown, six days a week, they hardly had enough to eat. In spite of this, they were happy because of their great love for one another.

But one year Simon, the younger brother, felt a great sadness.

His wife said, "Tell me what is making you so blue? You no longer sing while you work."

"You are right, dear wife. I am worried about my older brother, Ruben. He is alone in the world, with neither wife nor children. Who will care for him when he gets old and can no longer work? If only he had some money to save for his old age! It isn't fair that we share the harvest equally. But he is proud and will not accept gifts from me. What shall I do?"

"Would you take food from your own children?" she asked in astonishment. "There is nothing you can do," she said. "So forget it."

Simon knew that his wife was right, but he was determined to help Ruben.

Meanwhile, Ruben was sitting under a tree, thinking deeply. When he noticed a bird on the way to its winter home, he said, "That bird and I are fortunate because we are free. Neither of us has a wife and children always needing to be fed. But my poor brother, Simon, is burdened with a family.

"It isn't fair that we share the harvest equally. Surely he deserves more than I! But he is very proud and will not accept gifts from me. What can I do? In several days we take our harvest to town. If I don't think of a plan soon, it will be too late."

That night, when the moon was high in the heavens, Ruben went quietly to his barn where he filled a sack with wheat and put it on his shoulder. Then he crossed the empty field to his brother's hut and secretly placed his wheat with Simon's.

"Ah," he said when he had finished, "this is better. Now my dear younger brother will have more than I."

Ruben went happily back to his hut and slept soundly for the first time in weeks.

An hour later, Simon woke up with a start. He had dreamed of a marvelous plan. He crept out of bed, got dressed, and went to his barn. Filling a sack with wheat, walking across the field to Ruben's hut, and placing it there took very little time. Before long, he was back in bed, pulling up the covers.

"Now I can sleep peacefully," Simon thought aloud, "because Ruben will have a little extra to save for his old age."

The next morning Ruben and Simon were amazed. How could this be? Their piles of wheat were equal, yet each knew he had given wheat to the other. Something must have gone wrong.

So that night Ruben waited until midnight, when he again took Simon some of his grain. "There! Now I am fully awake, and I'm *sure* I put it on his pile. Tomorrow mine will be smaller and his larger, as it should be."

A short time later, Simon did the same. He, too, was sure that all would be well this time.

But when day dawned, each brother saw that his share was exactly half the harvest. Ruben and Simon were desperate. Tomorrow they were to go to town to sell their grain. Tonight was their last chance.

Midnight came again. But this time Ruben and Simon chose the same moment to carry out their mission of brotherly love. Each placed a sack of wheat on his shoulders and began to walk across the field. Halfway across they met.

"Ruben! What are you doing out so late at night?" cried Simon in dismay. He tried to hide his sack.

Startled, Ruben dropped his bundle. Then he saw Simon's sack, and they both began to laugh. When they finished laughing, they hugged each other tightly. Their hearts were full of love for each other, and they were content.

The Brocade Slipper

A Folk Story from Vietnam

Retold by Lynette Dyer Ti

In olden times there lived a man whose wife had died, leaving him with their only child, a beautiful daughter named Tam.

Sometime afterward the man married again. His second wife was a widow who also had a daughter of her own, an ugly ungainly girl named Cam.

In those days the husband's child was always considered the elder and received special privileges in everything. But Tam's stepmother was a cruel woman and hated Tam for her beauty and sweet disposition. Tam was forced to work long hours in the fields, tending the water buffaloes and feeding and caring for the other animals as well, while Cam spent the day lazily at home with her mother. Cam and her mother ate the good food, leaving only scraps for Tam.

Tam did not dare tell her father of the unjust treatment, for fear of her stepmother's beatings.

One day the stepmother called the two girls and said to them, "I don't know which of you to consider the elder, and I don't want to be accused of playing favorites, so I will let your own merits decide the matter. Here is a basket for each of you. Go down to the river and see how many fish you can catch. Whoever catches the most fish will be the elder."

The two girls set off together. When they reached the river, Tam set to work immediately, scooping up the fish with her hands and tossing them into her basket.

Cam lay down under a tree and went to sleep. Some time later she awoke and saw Tam's basket on the shore, full of fish. And her own basket, of course, was empty.

When Tam came up from the water, Cam exclaimed, "My, how muddy you are! You'd better take a bath before we go home."

Then, as soon as Tam was down in the water, Cam hurriedly poured all the fish into her own basket and ran home.

When Tam reached the house with her empty basket, her stepmother cried, "You lazy girl! Can't you ever do anything but play? Look at your sister's basket! It is full of fish. And yours does not even have a single one!"

Tam went back outside, still carrying her empty basket, and lay down on the grass and cried. Suddenly through her sobs she heard someone call her. Looking up, she saw a fairy.

"There, there, look in your basket," said the fairy.

Tam did as she was told. There lay a fat little fish.

"Put him in the water immediately," said the fairy, pointing toward the small pond behind the house. "He will bring you good luck. You must feed him every day. When you call him, he will come to you."

Every day Tam would set aside a portion of her meager dinner and slip away from the house and down to the little pond.

"Here, fish, fish, little fish," she would call.

As soon as he heard her voice, the little fish would come to the surface and eat the rice from her hand. Tam grew to love him, for he was her only friend.

One day Cam, wondering why her sister always hurried out of the house after dinner, followed her down to the pond and hid behind a tree to see what she would do. The next day when Tam was away tending the buffaloes, Cam went to the pond and, imitating Tam's voice, called the fish. When he came to the surface, she seized him and killed him. Once back in the house, she cooked the fish and ate it.

Later when Tam, her hands full of rice, came and called her fish, there was no answer.

Tears came to her eyes when she realized that something must have happened to him.

A rooster eating nearby started to crow loudly. "Cock-a-doodle-doo!" he called. "I'll find the bones for you."

He led Tam over to a pile of garbage and, scratching away, soon found the fish's bones for her. But when Tam saw the bones, she began to cry harder than ever.

"Don't cry, my child," a voice said.

Tam looked up and saw the fairy standing beside her.

"Listen to me, and do exactly as I say. Put the bones in a jar and hide it carefully under the head of your bed. Then after one hundred days, take out the jar and see what you find in it."

Tam went home immediately and did exactly as the fairy had instructed. One hundred days later she took out the jar and found to her amazement that it contained a pair of beautiful slippers brocaded in gold. She put the slippers on immediately. And from then on, whenever she left the house, she wore them.

One day, as she was driving the buffaloes to pasture, she stepped by accident into a mud puddle and dirtied her slippers. After washing them carefully, she placed them on the horns of one of the buffaloes to dry.

Suddenly a crow that was flying by took one of the slippers in his beak and flew off. Tam stood watching the bird until he was out of sight. There was no way for her to get her slipper back.

The crow flew on and on until he came to the capital. There, as he was flying over the royal palace, he dropped the slipper into the king's garden. The crown prince picked it up and examined its dainty shape and delicate pattern.

"This must belong to a lovely princess," he said. "What small, delicate feet she has! If only I could find her, I would make her my wife right away."

He sent out a proclamation declaring that whoever owned the mate to the slipper he had found would become his bride.

When Tam heard the news, she was filled with excitement. But her stepmother had noticed her missing slipper and had guessed what had happened. When Tam came to ask her permission to attend the celebration, she handed her two baskets full of sesame seeds.

"Before you go," she said, "I have a job for you. Take these two baskets and sort the seeds, the black seeds in one basket and the white seeds in the other. When you're finished, you can go."

Tam sat down in front of the baskets in despair. What was the use of even trying such an impossible task? She covered her face with her hands, and the tears flowed through her fingers.

Suddenly she felt something brush against her shoulder. Looking up, she saw that two pigeons had lighted on the rims of the baskets. They sorted out all the seeds. Tam took the baskets to her stepmother, who was so amazed that she could think of no other pretext for withholding her permission to go to the prince's celebration.

When Tam arrived at the palace and the prince saw that her slipper was exactly like the one he had found, he was so happy that he asked her to marry him at once.

The Message of the Nightingale

Retold by Bonnie Highsmith Taylor

There was once a king whose most prized possession was a nightingale.

The nightingale lived in the palace in a beautiful wire cage of pure silver. It drank water from a crystal bowl. It ate the finest seed grown in all the land from a diamond-studded dish.

Everywhere the king went in the palace he carried the cage. When he woke in the morning, the nightingale was beside his bed singing its magnificent song. When the king ate his meals in the royal dining hall, the nightingale sang beside him at the table. It sang for him while he bathed and while he sat in his royal throne.

"My nightingale wants for nothing," the king boasted to everyone. "I give it everything it needs. It does not have to hunt for food as other birds do. It does not have to face the cold, harsh winters as birds in the wild."

Yes, the king loved the nightingale very much.

One morning as the king filled the crystal bowl with water he said, "I must journey to the land beyond the river. But I will return soon."

"Oh, master," cried the nightingale. "I once lived in the land beyond the river. My brother lives there yet. Will you please take him a message?"

"I would be happy to," replied the king.

Said the nightingale, "You will find him at a garden of pomegranate trees with a stone wall around it. Tell him, kind sir, that I am loved and cared for by the kindest master in the world. And tell him that the cage I live in is of pure silver."

The king smiled proudly. "You may be sure I will deliver your message, my little friend."

"Please ask him if he has a message for me," said the nightingale.

The king promised, then left on his journey.

After he had finished his royal business, he went in search of the garden. It was days before he came to a lovely pomegranate grove inside a stone wall. Hundreds of birds sang gaily. But one sang more sweetly than the rest. *This must be the brother of my own dear bird,* thought the king.

"Oh, nightingale," he called out. "I have a message for you from your brother. He wishes you to know that he lives in luxury in my own palace. His cage is of pure silver. He wishes to know if you have a message for him."

Suddenly, the bird fell from the limb it was perched on and landed at the king's feet.

Surprised, the king knelt down and touched the bird. Its body was stiff. Its beak was open wide.

"Poor thing," the king sighed. "His envy was too much for him."

Thinking the nightingale dead, he threw him over the stone wall and left the garden.

But when the king was out of sight, the bird flew back to the limb and began to sing with all its might. Then it flew over the garden wall.

The king returned home.

"Oh, master," cried the nightingale. "Did you find my brother?"

Sadly the king replied, "Yes, little friend. But I fear your message was more than he could bear. In a spell of jealousy he dropped dead. "I threw the poor little thing over the garden wall."

The nightingale gasped. Its wings drooped.

All day it sat quietly, refusing food or water.

Not a note would it sing, though the king pleaded.

The very next morning when the king woke he rushed to the silver cage. The bird lay on the floor of the cage, lifeless.

The king picked it up and held it gently. Tears filled his eyes. "Poor, poor little one," he sobbed. "I should not have told you of your brother."

With a heavy heart the king carried the nightingale into the garden and threw it over the wall.

At once the nightingale fluttered its wings and flew to the top of a tall tree. "Thank you, master," it called down. "Thank you for the message you brought from my wise brother—for he has told me how to escape."

The king was dumbfounded. "But I do not understand. I gave you everything riches could buy."

"No, master," answered the nightingale. "Not everything. You gave me food, shelter, and loving care. But you did not give me the greatest gift of all. My freedom."

Many times after that the king heard the nightingale singing in the nearby woods.

"In the silver cage," the king said, "he never sang so sweetly."

The Caliph
and the
Widow

An Arabian Folktale

Retold by Bahija Lovejoy

Many, many years ago there lived in Arabia a caliph whose name was Omar. He was known for his justice and the love he had for his people. Every morning he sat on a big divan that served as a throne. Near him stood his ministers and advisers. Then the gates of the palace would open wide. Everybody, rich or poor, regardless of religion or color, was allowed in. As each person entered, the great leader would listen to his problems. If the person needed help, the caliph found ways to solve the problems.

Everybody loved this wonderful father of the people. "How great is Omar!" they would cry. "He is a good shepherd to his people."

Did I say everybody loved him? Well, I was wrong! Out in the desert many Bedouins lived in black tents made of goat's hair. One of these did not love the caliph. This person was a poor widow who lived in one of the black tents with her three children.

One night the widow stood before a small fire upon which a pot was boiling. On the floor the three children huddled together, crying and begging for food.

The mother stirred the pot with a large wooden spoon. Her face was thin and tired. Her voice sounded sad. "Be patient, my children. Be patient."

Crying like small lambs, the children, exhausted and weak, fell asleep. Outside, the howling wind blew the flap of the tent aside. As the widow moved to close it, she gave a startled cry. Two men were standing there, dressed in the rough clothing of poor shepherds.

"What is it? What do you want of me?" cried the frightened woman.

"Peace be with you, sister," said the older of the two men. "Tell me, why were the children crying?"

"They are hungry," she answered.

The man looked angrily at the pot still boiling on the fire. He could see round white vegetables in it.

"Why don't you serve them some of that food?" he demanded.

The woman sighed. A tear rolled down her brown cheek as she whispered, "There is no food in the pot."

The older man turned to his companion. "Abbas, see what is in the pot."

Abbas took the wooden spoon from the woman's hand and dipped it into the pot. To his great surprise the pot was filled with stones and pebbles!

The trembling woman spoke. "I am a widow. I have no relatives or friends. My husband left us very little. Today I had no food to give them so I pretended to the children that the stones were vegetables for soup. I was going to give them the hot water and tell them that it was broth. However, as you see, they have fallen asleep."

"Why did you not ask the caliph Omar for help?" asked the older shepherd.

"Please do not speak to me of Omar," she said. "I would rather die with my children than stretch my hand for alms. I am a poor woman, but I shall never beg from the caliph. The caliph is a shepherd to his people. He is supposed to look after his flock. This he has not done when a widow and her children are left to starve."

"You are right, sister. What you have said is true," replied the older shepherd. "The caliph has done an injustice to you and your children!" He pulled his hood up over his head. "Wait here. We shall return in a short time."

As the two men hurried away, Abbas heard his friend saying over and over under his breath, "How can such a thing exist while Omar is the caliph?" They disappeared toward the town that lay nestled at the edge of the desert. After a short time had passed, they returned, carrying large bundles on their backs. They went to the tent and placed near the fire the food they had brought.

"Now, sister, let us throw away these stones. Abbas will gather more brush and camel dung for the fire. We shall prepare good food for the children and for you."

The woman was too full of amazement to answer. She watched the men fill the pot with food. The older man sat by the fire. The other one stirred with the big wooden spoon. When the food was cooked, the man who sat by the fire said, "Sister, you can awaken the children now."

The mother poured the food onto a big copper tray and put it on the floor by the children. They smiled in their sleep as they smelled the delicious stew. Then they were suddenly wide-awake.

"Children," said the shepherd by the fire, "your mother promised you dinner and here it is."

The little ones laughed and filled up their tiny bowls again and again as they ate.

"Oh, Mother, how good it is!" they cried.

When they had filled their stomachs with the delicious food, they tumbled happily together and went to sleep like contented puppies.

The two men rose to go. They were smiling because the sight of the children had made them happy. The mother still had tears in her eyes, but now they were tears of joy.

"I want to thank you for what you have done," she cried. "The caliph Omar would never have helped me. He would never know that a poor widow like me is even alive."

"Sister, I believe that you are wrong about the caliph," said the older shepherd. "He, too, is a shepherd, and he is concerned about each one of his sheep. He will see to it that you and your children will never go hungry again. You must trust him." With these words he left the tent.

The puzzled widow turned to Abbas. "How can that shepherd say I am wrong about the caliph? He saw, as you did, that I had nothing," she said.

"He can say that, my sister, because the shepherd who just left your tent is Omar. The caliph himself has prepared your dinner this night!" Abbas smiled, bowed, and then left the tent.

The Boxfish
and the
Flounder

A Polynesian Folktale

Retold by Marion E. Dixon

The boxfish and the flounder were both ashamed of the way they looked.

They watched the long, sleek shark shoot through the water. They watched the beautiful butterfly fish flash by. They watched the silvery salmon sparkle in and out of the waves. And they felt very sad and ugly.

"I'll fix you up if you'll fix me up," said the fat, floppy flounder to the baggy, bulgy boxfish.

"Wonderful!" cried the boxfish. "Then let us start right away!"

The flounder shaped and smoothed the first side of the boxfish until it was straight and shiny, and then he turned him over.

The flounder shaped and smoothed the second side of the boxfish until it was straight and shiny, and then he turned him over again.

The flounder fixed the third side of the boxfish until it, too, was straight and shiny, and then he turned him over a third time.

The flounder stopped working for a minute to rest, and the boxfish said, "You won't forget to do my last side, will you?"

The boxfish always worried about others forgetting things because *he* was so forgetful. If someone said good morning to him, he often forgot to say good morning back.

But the flounder didn't forget the boxfish's fourth side. He shaped and polished it until the boxfish looked perfect.

"Look at your reflection," said the flounder to the boxfish.

The boxfish looked and looked. He thought he looked just right. His head and fins and tail were in the best possible places, and his body was smooth and boxy the way he'd always wanted it. Now he could swim where everyone could see him instead of hiding behind a rock.

"It's my turn now," the flounder said to the boxfish. "Make me look as handsome as you do."

So the boxfish started to work on the flounder. He worked very hard, smoothing and flattening out the flounder's lumpy body.

But he forgot to turn the flounder over. He just kept smoothing and flattening one side of the flounder until he was exhausted. He said that was all he could do, and he told the flounder to look at his reflection.

The flounder looked and looked. Both of his eyes were on one side of his body, and his mouth was badly twisted. His body was as thin and flat as a big piece of seaweed. The forgetful boxfish had spoiled him completely.

The flounder was so upset that he hid in the sand at the bottom of the ocean where no one could see him. He felt even more ashamed and miserable than before.

Then one day he looked up and saw a group of sharks thrashing through the water, gobbling up all the fish that came their way. The boxfish barely escaped, leaving behind the tip of his tail in a greedy shark's mouth.

The flounder lay very still, so well covered that only his moving eyes could be seen. The sharks passed right over him without seeing him.

"I am glad I was not swimming up there like the boxfish," he said. "The sharks would have had me for supper."

He snuggled a little deeper into the sand. It was clear that there were other misfortunes worse than his. So the forgetful boxfish had done him a favor after all!

The Carambola Tree

Adapted from a Vietnamese Story

By John M. Zielinski

Near the village of Bich Cau in the land of Van Lang that is today Vietnam, there once lived two orphan brothers. They worked very hard on the land that their father had left in the care of his eldest son. Both brothers grew up and got married. Then the elder one became lazy and left all the hard work to his younger brother and sister-in-law.

The young couple did not mind. They worked day and night, plowing and caring for the land.

Soon the young couple were growing more than the two brothers had been able to grow before.

The older brother grew afraid that the younger would want most of the crop. He decided to move them off his land, so he gave them a little thatched cottage with a carambola tree before it. They did not cry at their loss but went into the forest to gather firewood to sell in the market, and they worked as laborers in the fields of others.

Their happiest days were when the carambola fruit was ripe, for then they had enough to eat. All year round they took great care of the tree, keeping the ants and other insects away. It rewarded them with cool green shade and an abundance of fruit, even on its lowest branches.

One morning when the couple was getting ready to pick the fruit, they saw the tree shaking violently. Looking up, they saw a large, strange bird eating the ripe fruit. They waited patiently for him to finish before picking any for themselves.

The bird came every morning for a month. It sat calmly in the tree until it had eaten its fill, then flew away.

Finally the woman spoke to it. "Dear bird, if you keep eating like that, there will soon be none left."

The bird looked down at her and answered, "A gold coin for each fruit eaten! Make a bag three spans long to contain the gold." He repeated these words three times and flew away.

The husband and wife were very surprised to hear the bird speak, but they did as it told them.

The following morning a strong wind shook the cottage, and the huge bird landed in the middle of the yard. The husband went out with the bag. The bird instructed him to climb up on its back. When the man had done this, the bird stretched its neck and took off.

The journey was long—sometimes over silvery clouds, sometimes over huge green forests and red mountains and, at last, over the vast ocean.

Suddenly, an island appeared below. It was bathed in a dazzling light as many white, blue, and red stones reflected the sun. The bird circled the island as if searching for a place to land. At last it perched on a small level spot a short way from the mouth of a cave.

The bird told the man to go into the cave and take what he wanted. There were many crystal stones and much gold and silver lying around the entrance. The man was afraid to go into the cave because he might get lost. So he quickly picked up a small quantity of gold and diamonds, put them in his bag, and climbed once again onto the bird's back.

The bird was happy. Its cries echoed from the rocks as it took off. Across ocean, forest, and mountains they traveled. At noon they were once again in the yard before the cottage.

The wife ran out of the house and saw that her husband was safe. She hugged the bird and told it to help itself to the fruit. When the bird had eaten, it saluted them with three cries and flew away. From that day on, it came only now and then to eat the fruit.

Rumor of the young couple's wealth quickly spread, and the elder brother and his wife now hurried to visit the younger brother. After hearing the story, the elder brother begged him to exchange his thatched hut and carambola tree for the farm. The young couple accepted gladly.

Each morning the elder brother and his wife stretched lazily beneath the carambola tree, awaiting the arrival of the bird.

One morning they were awakened by a great gust of wind, which shook the roof of the house. They rushed out to see the huge bird sitting on the tree eating the fruit.

When it had eaten a little, the wife cried, "We have only this tree. How can we live if you eat fruit like a wolf?"

The bird answered as before.

The man and wife argued all night about the size of the bag. They wanted to make several bags, but they were afraid the bird might be angry. So instead they made one, three times as large as the younger brother's.

The next morning the bird came, and the husband climbed up on its back. The bird flew once again to the island.

The man was dazzled by the glittering, multicolored stones. Once inside the cave, he forgot his hunger and thirst and worked feverishly to fill his bag. He also tied the ends of his pants and his coat sleeves, and filled them with gold and diamonds. When he finished, he could scarcely drag himself to the cave entrance, so heavy was his burden.

The bird uttered cries of impatience. But it was afternoon before the man could drag the bag to where the bird waited. To keep the bag from falling, he tied it firmly beneath the bird's wings.

The bird tried to fly but was so weighted down it could only skim over the ground. It exerted more effort and finally succeeded in flying. The man was dreaming of the huge palace he would build. He and his wife would never have to work another day.

While he was thinking, the bird was flying over the ocean. The weather changed; the blue waves grew gray and became larger and larger. Flying against the wind, the bird became very tired. Its wings began to tremble. The winds caused the heavy bag to bump against its wings. As the bird began to falter and sink toward the sea, the rope broke and the bag fell. The man cried out and reached to grab it. In an instant both man and bag were gone. With his pants and coat sleeves full of gold and diamonds, he sank like a stone.

The bird skimmed along the water. Gaining strength, it rose and flew away toward the mountains and forest.

A Hundred Cows To Milk

By Bonnie Highsmith Taylor

Long ago in the faraway village of Dork there lived a maiden. She was young and fair and her name was Pernella.

Pernella lived with her mother and father and her seven sisters. They were very poor.

Though the father loved Pernella and her seven sisters, he was anxious for them to marry. He was poor and he knew that he could not care for them much longer.

He said to Pernella, "You are the eldest, therefore you should marry first."

Pernella wanted to marry. She wanted to marry a man who was handsome, gentle, and jolly. Such a man would make a good husband.

There were two men who wanted to marry Pernella. There was Zebulon, and there was Godfrey.

Zebulon was handsome, gentle, and jolly. He lived in a small cottage. He had a small plot of land. He worked hard, and he loved Pernella. But he was very poor.

Godfrey, on the other hand, was not *quite* so handsome. Not *quite* so gentle. Not *quite* so jolly.

But it was said that Godfrey was quite wealthy. It was said that he had a grand house with fine things inside. It was said that he had a very large plot of land. But best of all, it was said that he had a HUNDRED cows to milk!

Pernella's father had not even *one* cow to milk. Zebulon had not even *one* cow to milk.

A man with a hundred cows to milk was very, very rich.

"A hundred cows to milk!" said Pernella's father. "Keep that in mind."

"He must be very rich," said Pernella's mother.

"Very rich indeed!" said her seven sisters.

"A hundred cows to milk!" said everyone in the village. "What a rich man!"

Still Pernella could not make up her mind.

Though Zebulon was oh so handsome and oh so gentle and oh so jolly, he was also oh so poor.

Though Godfrey was only a *little* handsome, a *little* gentle, and a *little* jolly, he was oh so rich.

Zebulon begged and pleaded with Pernella to marry him. Godfrey begged and pleaded with Pernella to marry him.

"Think it over," said her father and mother. "One hundred cows makes a very rich man."

"Godfrey must be oh so rich," said Pernella's seven sisters. "Think it over."

Pernella did think it over. And think it over. And think it over. But still she could not make up her mind.

Then one fine morning Godfrey came calling. He came calling in a shiny black coach pulled by a shiny black horse.

"Come with me, Pernella," he said. "Let me show you what I have to give a wife."

Away they rode in the shiny black coach pulled by the shiny black horse.

They were gone for a long time. When Pernella finally got back home, she said to her father and mother and seven sisters, "I have made up my mind. I will marry Zebulon."

"But what about Godfrey?" asked her father. "Did he not have a grand house with fine things?"

"Did he not have a large plot of land?" asked her mother.

"Did he not have a hundred cows to milk?" asked her seven sisters.

Pernella smiled. "Oh, yes," she said. "It is all true. Godfrey has a grand house with fine things. He has a large, large plot of land. And he does have a hundred cows to milk."

"Then you should be happy to marry him," said her father. "A rich man needs a good wife."

"Godfrey does not need a good wife," said Pernella. "He needs someone to milk a hundred cows. And it shall not be I!"

So Pernella married Zebulon, because he was oh so handsome, oh so gentle, and oh so jolly. And because they loved each other oh so much.

And even though Zebulon did not have a hundred cows to milk, they lived happily ever after.